CHEETAHS

Amelie von Zumbusch

PowerKiDS press™

Published in 2007 by The Rosen Publishing Group, Inc.
29 East 21st Street, New York, NY 10010

First Edition

Book Design: Erica Clendening
Layout Design: Julio Gil

Photo Credits: Cover, pp. 1, 9, 11, 17, 19, 23, 24 (top left, top right, bottom right) © Digital Vision; p. 5 © Artville; pp. 7, 13, 15, 21, 24 (bottom left) © Digital Stock.

Library of Congress Cataloging-in-Publication Data

Zumbusch, Amelie von.
  Cheetahs / Amelie von Zumbusch. — 1st ed.
     p. cm. — (Safari animals)
  Includes bibliographical references and index.
  ISBN-13: 978-1-4042-3614-1 (library binding)
  ISBN-10: 1-4042-3614-7 (library binding)
  1. Cheetah—Juvenile literature. I. Title.
  QL737.C23Z79 2007
  599.75'9—dc22
                                                      2006019453

Manufactured in the United States of America

CONTENTS

Cheetahs are members of the cat family. They sometimes purr as house cats do.

5

The cheetah is the fastest animal on Earth. Cheetahs can run as fast as 70 miles per hour (113 km/hr).

A cheetah's coat is covered with black spots. Cheetahs have a black stripe on each side of their nose.

9

Cheetahs have small heads and thin bodies. This helps them run fast.

Most cheetahs live on the savannahs of Africa.

13

Cheetahs eat meat. They run fast to catch animals for food.

Many cheetahs live alone. Others live in small family groups.

Cheetah cubs are born with gray fur on their backs. They get spots when they are a few months old.

19

Young cheetahs live with their mothers until they are between one and two years old.

21

There are not many cheetahs left in the wild. There are some parks where they can live safely, though.

Words to Know

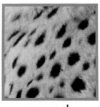

coat

cubs

savannah

stripe

Index

Web Sites

Due to the changing nature of Internet links, PowerKids Press has developed an online list of Web sites related to this book. This site is updated regularly. Please use this link to access the list: www.powerkidslinks.com/safari/cheetah/

24